The ADVENTURES OF

MUNNIE BUTTERFLY & DANNY Dragonfly

I the SKY & Me the SEA

KRIS RAMPERSAD

MUNNIE
MultiCultural
Musical
Masquerade

Book One

Leaves of Life
FESTIVAL FABLES

The Adventures of Munnie Butterfly & Danny Dragonfly

Book 1: I the Sky & Me the Sea

Cover designed by Kris Rampersad.

Munnie & Danny Design Concept & Creator: Jolie Wong

Page Layout and Designs and Photography by Kris Rampersad

Others in this Series: Book 2: The Great Green One-Eyed GIANT

Book 3: Munnie's MultiCultural Musical Masquerade

Published by

Dr Kris Rampersad/Leaves of Life

St Augustine, Trinidad and Tobago

www.KrisRampersad.com, lolleaves@gmail.com

ISBN-978-976-8228-11-6

The ADVENTURES OF MUNNIE BUTTERFLY & DANNY Dragonfly

I the SKY & Me the SEA

KRIS RAMPERSAD

MUNNIE MultiCultural Musical Masquerade

Book One

FROM THE AUTHOR

Stories were the first form of journalism in my neck of the woods. My father told us stories that he spun from his imagination night after night when we were children growing up in a rural district in the Caribbean. I hope these revive family and community storytime and other activities, even while they integrate new technologies with multimedia animation, musical and dramatized versions. The story of Munnie and her world of travels began unfolding as I wrote for my nephew, Saiesh, when he was only three years old. I found it difficult to convey in reading the realities of many of the mainly foreign offerings of available children's books, to stimulate his creativity and imagination triggered by the world with which he was familiar. He was its first critic and grew into an avid reader. His enthusiastic reception and wish for more inspired these Fables. Over the last decade, these Munnie stories inspired other children in oral traditions of storytime, theatre workshops, playtime at the park, at vacation camps and in my activities as an independent educator and journalist trying to stimulate interests in reading and cultural heritage. The purpose then, as now, is to integrate entertainment with education across disciplines of arts and sciences, environment and culture nurturing curiosity while encouraging appreciation of diversity, intergenerational respect, value and appreciation of each other and the world around us. Subscribe to my website www.krisrampersad.com for new ways of using these stories, new learnings forms and to participate in interactive sessions, with new activities and exciting online and events and other vital information releases.

ABOUT THE AUTHOR

DR KRIS RAMPERSAD is an award-winning international author, educator and journalist. She holds a PhD in Literatures in English, teaches the literatures of Europe, Africa, Asia, the Americas and the Caribbean in English and is a UNESCO-trained cultural heritage expert facilitator who has explored many lands and worked with people from many different cultures. She facilitated the first UNESCO Caribbean Youth Workshop in Intangible Cultural Heritage and served as President of the UNESCO Education Commission, piloting the Global Agenda for Education for the next generations. Her special interests are experiencing and presenting the rich and vibrant multicultural and interconnected global heritage to children from ages 3 to 103. She is the author of highly-acclaimed books, *Finding A Place, Through the Political Glass Ceiling* and *LiTTscapes, Landscapes of Fiction*.

These new delightful Festival Fables explore our interconnected living heritage and tangible and intangible environments in novel ways. They tell of our linkages to each other and to nature, through our natural and cultural heritage. They make learning fun with an integrated approach to many disciplines as numeracy, literacy, sciences, the arts and in exploration o fantasy and reality.

I the Sky & Me the Sea, the first book in the series sets the tone, as the landscapes and mindscapes the series covers will be everything between the Sky & Sea, & add to that some sensational singalongs! Look for more in this multimedia series with animation and music, and interactive workbooks and primers. Participate in stimulating sessions with the author. To make a request or to keep track of exciting new releases subscribe to: www.krisrampersad.com.

MY NEPHEWS, NIECES
& The Next Generations Who Light My Path

For whom these stories are written;
My nephew Saiesh, the first reader and critic;
Pa who filled our rustic nights with stories;
Ma who inspires the journey onwards & the
Next Generations as they carry on the legacy of
Our ancestors who travelled across many seas
to make us part of this monumental
Mystical, Magical, Multicultural Milieu.

TABLE OF CONTENTS

Book 1:
I the SKY & Me the SEA

MUNNIE FOLLOWS THE MUSIC

Tumtumtumtumtitumtitumtum
Munnie's wings flutter in the wind.
Tumtitumtumtitumtitumboomboom
Her antennae pick up sweet sounds.
What are these sounds?
Her wings flutter in time with the sounds.
BoomTumTumtiBoomBoomtumtiboom.
Munnie tries to keep her four wings still.
She tries to straighten her two antennae.
Why do they always curl up when she
wants to hear the sounds better?
The sounds drift up towards her.
TumTumtitumboomboomtiboomtitumBoom
They fill strands of wind with music.
Munnie's wings flutter in time to the sounds.
Tumtitumtitumtiboomshakalacabumtitum.

FAIRY FRIEND FOE OR FAMILY?

Munnie looks down. Below is a vast ocean of sparkling greeny-blue. It is like the space between her eyes. The sparkling water dazzles her. It looks like a large bed of sparkling diamonds! A pair of wispy wings hover over the ocean. Munnie moves closer to better admire the wings.

They are so wispy she can see right through them. They sparkle, like the water below. She wonders:
Are these the wings of an Ocean Fairy? Friend? Foe?
Or can this be Family?

The wings are all the colours of the rainbow and more. Munnie names the colours. They are the same colours in her wings. They are different shades of the same colours. Are these beautiful wings making these sounds? "Where am I, in heaven? Are you an angel?" Munnie whispers to the wispy whispering wings.

"What beautiful wings you have! They make my four wings look heavy!" Munnie moves closer.

What a surprise she gets!
Orange. Yellow Green
Red Purple White
Black Blue Pink

3

MUSICAL FLAIRS IN THE AIR

The angel wings are moving towards her!
The angel wings begin to speak!
It is a beautiful musical sound too!
It adds a musical flair to the air.
TingTingTitititingtitingting.
The wispy fairy-like creature
laughs. "Your wings are very
beautiful, too. I am a Dragonfly.
Danny at your service, Miss." The
beautiful creature bows.

Danny Dragonfly flutters his
gossamer wings. Danny's
gossamer wings make music
too. *TingTingTitititingtiting.*
It blends with the sounds of
music in the air.

4

A-FLITTER AND A-FLUTTER

"You look lost," says Danny Dragonfly.
"I am a little bit lost," Munnie admits.
"I left my friends in the hollow tree in the cold winter of the lands up North. I was so bored in the cold winter all day and all night so I came out for a flutter."

"Well, you fluttered very far," says Danny with a laugh and a flitter-flutter of his own. FliTTingtingtititingtititingtiting.

"I told my friends, 'I am going to fly far, far out. I will fly to the line where the sea touches the sky. It will be warmer there.' They laughed at me," says Munnie sadly.

Danny's wings go: Tingtitin

SPLISH! SPLASH! Splish Splash goes the Sea

Munnie's wings go Tumtitum titumtum

5

SQUIGGLY GROUCH AND FROGO

'HaHaHaHaAhAhA Fly far away, and get squashed?' Grouchy Groundhog growled. 'I prefer to sleep all winter.' He crawled onto a leaf and fell fast asleep.

'How far can you go with your girly wings?' squealed Squiggly Squirrel.

He stomped on the ground, snorting so hard he nearly choked as he was nibbling on a nut.

They made her friend Frogo Frog frown. He wanted to join her. He tried to fly away with her but frogs have no wings! She left him on land.

"My name is Munnie. I am a butterfly. You look like me. You look like a butterfly, but you do not look like my family," Munnie says to Danny Dragonfly. Danny flits out of the Sea with a **SPLISH SPLISH SPLASH!**

TingtingTitititingtitingting. Danny's gossamer wings make music too. Munnie and Danny flit and flutter to hear the sounds their wings make together. Tumtitumtitumtum, goes Munnie's wings. Danny's wings go: **Tingtingtiting.**

Munnie's wings go
TumtitumTitumtum

Danny's wings
go: Tingtiting

The Sea goes Splish Splash **SPLISH SPLASHH!**

FRIENDS OF FLIGHT

The new friends gaze at each other. They notice they are the same. "We are both insects. We can fly," Danny says, flitting a flitter around her. "We have heads, thorax, and abdomen." says Munnie, lifting her wings to show her thorax. "We have four wings, many eyes and two antennae," Danny flutters. "I can see we both have two main eyes and many eyes on our wings."

"We are different too. Your wings are longer, more flimsy," says Munnie, fluttering around Danny. "I am born and live near land. Your main eyes are larger and you have many more eyes on your wings than I on mine."

"They help us see more beauty in the world," Danny says. "I spend more time near water. I was born near water."

The Sea goes Splish Splash SPLISH SPLASHH!

THE FASTEST FLITTER-COPTER

"Your wings flit and flitter so much faster than mine," says Munnie.

"You mean like this?" Danny asks. He twists his thorax. Round and round goes Danny Dragonfly.
"You are like the fastest flit-flitter-copter!" Munnie exclaims.
Tumtitumtum goes her wings excitedly.
TingtingTititititingtitingting goes Danny's wings as he flits around like the fastest flitter-copter. He moves his body and head and thorax, around and around.
He darts in and out of the ocean.
"Show off!" Munnie flutters. "You are the fastest flitter-copter I know."
"For your entertainment!" he chuckles.

The Ocean-Sea goes Splish Splash SPLISH SPLASHH!

SUNNY SMILES SHINE IN THE SEA

Munnie is happy to make a new friend. She is glad to be far from the cold! She spreads her wings to feel the smiles of the warm Sun. It is so warm and bright, here. She says: "How my cold winter friends would regret they did not follow me!"

"Those land creatures! They made you sad and blue. How they would turn green with envy now if they knew reached the sun," says Danny. He is beaming as bright as the sun. He wants to cheer her up so her sunny smile too shines into the sea. "Here, blue and green are happy colours," Munnie laughs. I am happy to be in a different world." She could still hear the music. Her heart flutters at the beauty all around her: the blue sky up above and the greeny-blue ocean down below. She asks in awe: "Where am I? Is this heaven?"

The Ocean-Sea goes SPLISH! SPLASH! Splish Splash

A-TUNING AND A-TURNING

"Yes. This is awesome! It is just like heaven, as we folks from these parts say. I will show you! I will be your guide," says Munnie's new friend, Danny Dragonfly. "Find your flutter and follow me, little butterfly."
Munnie flutters her girly wings in glee. She turns and tunes her antennae towards the sounds. She listens. She tries to hear the sounds over the flut-fluttering of her four wings. TumtitumtiTumtititum.
She tries to hear the music over the flitter-flittering of Danny's four wings. TingtingTitingtingtumTingtingtitum
She tries to hear the music above the splish splashing of the deep blue Sea. BoomboomshacalakatumtitumBOOMTUMtum.

11

VENTURE TO ADVENTURE

"Listen," Danny says.
Tumtumtitumboomtum
Boomboomshacalaka
TumboomtumtiTumTum

"I followed those sounds here.
That music sounds like our wings.
What is making this beautiful sound?"
Munnie asks.
Danny smiles mischievously. "You ventured out of
your cold winter land over the ocean to look for
adventure in our warm sea. Well, you have come to
the right place, little butterfly!" Danny gives her
wing a gentle tug. "Try to catch up with me if you
can, my friend!" He flits off, so fast that Munnie
could barely see him in the distance.
"Wait for me," she calls. With a sudden flitting he is
already almost out of sight and far ahead of her.

SUN SEA AND SKY

They flit and flutter in the warm
blue sky, high above the deep blue
Sea. Over the water and under the smiling Sun,
the two Best Flitter Flutter Friends flitter and flutter.
Danny spreads his wings. He tries to hold both the
sea and the sky between his wings.
His wings go: Tingtititingtingtiting.
He says: "We are in the Caribbean.
Below us, see the blue Caribbean Sea.
Above us, behold the blue Caribbean sky!"

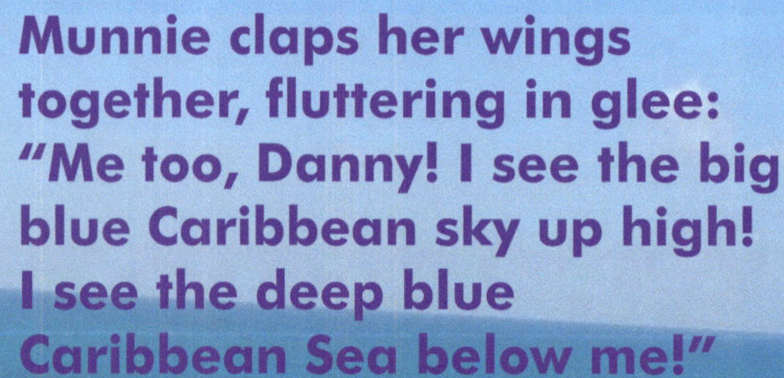

Munnie claps her wings
together, fluttering in glee:
"Me too, Danny! I see the big
blue Caribbean sky up high!
I see the deep blue
Caribbean Sea below me!"

The Sea goes: Splish Splash SPLISH SPLASHH!

13

RAPSO MIX UP ABOVE DOWN BELOW

Munnie turns to Danny. "I am a little bit confused. You are so wise. Can you explain this to me? Both the Sea and the Sky are big and blue but they are not the same. They are different." Munnie waits patiently for a response.

Danny gets thoughtful as he replies. "I have seen many, many suns and moons. I hear the Sky and the Sea when they sing." His wings flit out a melody. "It is a rapso rhythm mix up from these parts," he says. Munnie listens carefully, fluttering in time to his flitting. Danny continues: "The Sky is up, above. The Sea is down, below. The Sea is a mirror for the smiles of the Sky. The Sky knows where it is. Why? When it sees the Sea, below. The Sea knows it is down below because it sees the Sky up above. They would not know who they are without each other. The Sea gets grey and sad if the Sky is grey and sad. The Sea turns a happy blue, if the Sky is happy too. They are like us, same, but different."

"Same difference," the friends say at the same time, flitting and fluttering together. They laugh heartily.

SHADES OF SAME AND DIFFERENT

"In our world too, there are many different sounds of music and many shades of the same colours," Munnie says sagely. They flit and flutter to where the Sea and Sky join heads. "Can you hear what they are saying?" Munnie whispers. The BFFFs turn their antennae and tune them to listen closely.

Danny whispers: "The Sea and the Sky always meet at the Horizon Line. They remind each other that no matter how much distance or difference there is between them they will always meet at the Horizon.

At the Horizon the Sea and Sky share everything they find, everything they see and everything they learn so they will always be equal. They are best friends. Sometimes a rainbow joins them, to sip the wisdom of the Sky and the Sea." Danny tilts his head and bows to the bent multicoloured Rainbow. Munnie gazes at the straight Horizon.

Munnie
gazes
at the
straight
Horizon

Danny bows to the
bent rainbow

15

BFFFS-BEST FLITTER-FLUTTER FRIENDS

"Can we be best friends too Danny? The Sea and the Sky are both blue. They are different colours of blue. They are like us. We are the same species and we are different shades of same colours. I like the Sky," Munnie flutters a-flut. "And I like the Sea," Danny flits. "Yes. We are the same, but different. We are like the Sea and the Sky. We can be best friends like the Sea and the Sky," Danny hums. Tingtitingtitum. Munnie hums: TumTiTumTiTum. The two best flittering fluttering friends celebrate their new friendship across Sea and Sky.

The Sea and Sky begin to hum. The Sun shines a smile from the Sky onto the Sea. The Rainbow joins the show. In chips the chirpy Horizon, in unison. The two best flittering fluttering friends join Sky and Sea, singing the songs of I and Me.

Danny and Munnie flitter and flutter and sing-along with I the Sky and Me the Sea

Splish Splash SPLISH SPLASHH!
Sighs the Sea to the silent Sky.
Splish Splash SPLISH SPLASH with me,
Oh Sky up high.
Splish Splash SPLISH SPLASH with me,
The deep blue Sea.
See what I, the Sea, have seen, Oh Sky!
Shouts the Sea to the silent Sky, up high
Splish Splash SPLISH SPLASH with me,
Oh Sky, up high
Splish Splash SPLISH SPLASH with me, the Sea."

Danny flits a-flitter in glee as he sings
the Sea song Splish Splash With Me
The Sea.

Splish Splash With Me, The Sea
SONG OF THE SEA *TO THE SILENT SKY*

Listen to where I have been, Dear Sky, up high
Sighs the Sea to the silent Sky.
Splish Splash SPLISH SPLASH with me, Oh Sky, up high
Splish Splash SPLISH SPLASH with me, the Sea.
I go from shore to shore, near and far, far and near
from home, I go,
Sings the Sea to the silent Sky.
I have been beyond the Horizon;
Played with Rainbows too, have you?
Sings the Sea to the silent Sky, up high!
Oh Sky, up high,
Splish Splash SPLISH SPLASH with me, the Sea,
Sings the Sea to the silent Sky up high.
Splish Splash SPLISH SPLASH with me, Oh Sky, up high
Splish Splash SPLISH SPLASH with me, the Sea.

See What I the Sky, Spy, Up High
SONG OF I, THE SKY, UP HIGH
TO THE SPLISHING SPLASHING SEA

"Shhhhhhhhhhhhhhhhhhhhhhhhhhhhhhhh
Sigh no more, my friend, Dear Sea,"
Whispers the Sky from high to the sighing Sea!
"In silence you will hear, Oh Sea, a softer melody.
Shhhhhhhhhhhhhhhhhhhhhhhhhhhhhhhh
Listen with I, the Sky, O Sea,
To the breath of the wind, near me, hear…."
Sings the Sky up high to the splashing Sea!
"Shhhhhhhhhhhhhhhhhhhhhhhhhhhhhhhh
And you would hear, Oh Sea
The wind on wings of all creatures dear,
To you the Sea, and I, the Sky up high.
Shhhhhhhhhhhhhhhhhhhhhhhhhhhhhhhh
Listen to what I, the Sky, spy, up high. O Sea!"
Sings the Sky to the splishing Sea.
"Hear with me, the humming heavens,
a mesmerising melody. Shhhhhhhhhhh."

Munnie syncs her flutters in unison with the straight
Horizon, singing the Song of I the Sky, Up High.

See What I Spy from the Sky Up High
SONG OF THE SKY *TO THE SPLASHING SEA*

Shhhhhhhhhhhhhhhhhhhhhhhhhhhhhhhhhhh
"Splish Splash no more and you hear, Dear Sea
Moods of many moons, suns, stars, near me,
Here, up high, by I, the Sky."
Sings the Sky on high to the splashing Sea!
"Shhhhhhhhhhhhhhhhhhhhhhhhhhhhhh
 "Listen to the murmuring trees, the humming
Birds, the buzzing bees, Dear Sea, hear.
Shhhhhhhhhhhhhhh. Dear Sea,
What wonders I spy, from the Sky up high,"
Sings the Sky to the splish-splashing Sea.
"See beyond the beauteous bended Rainbow,
Across the narrow, thin and straight Horizon line
Shhhhhhhhhhhhhhhhhhhhhhhhhhhhhhhh,
Dear Sea. Hear what I, the Sky, high up here
Do hear, Shhhhhhh" Sings the Sky up high
To the splishing-splashing deep blue Sea.
Shhhhhhhhhhhhhhhhhhhhhhhhhhhhhhhhhh

BFFFS OF THE SEA & SKY

Still humming, as they flitter and flutter, Danny
Dragonfly says to Munnie Butterfly:
"I like to splish splash with the Sea. Watch me."
His wings sigh with the Sea as he dives down into
the sparkling blue water. "Come! Splish Splash
with me! Munnie," he calls.
"I like to fly, high up to the Sky," Munnie Butterfly
laughs. "Watch me fly to the sky, way up high.
Come Danny, my friend, join me!"
 Danny and Munnie say together at the same
time. "We are same, but different!" They laugh.
"Same difference." The two BFFF's Danny and
Munnie grin and fly, flitter and flutter between
Sea and Sky beneath as the smiling sun look on.

21

BUMPITY BUMP BUMP

Singing, soaring and sighing, the two Best Flitting and Fluttering Friends are so engrossed in singing the songs of Me and I of the Sea and Sky that they forget themselves. Bumpity Bump! BUMP! BUMP! "Watch out!" Munnie screams. Too late! "Look Danny. It's a Great Green Giant!" Munnie shouts. They both bump into the **Great Green One-Eyed Giant** of the Deep Blue Sea. What happens next? We will see! They will keenly interest you & me. These novel adventures of Munnie & Danny.

More in Books 2 & 3 Next in the SERIES

THE GREAT GREEN GIANT
Of the Deep Blue Sea

22

The ADVENTURES OF
MUNNIE BUTTERFLY & DANNY DRAGONFLY
The GREAT GREEN
Book 2
MUNNIE
MultiCultural
Musical
Masquerade
ONE-EYED GIANT
LoL
Leaves of Life
FESTIVAL FABLES
KRIS RAMPERSAD
www.krisrampersad.com
KnowLedgePot
LEAVES OF LIFE GLOBAL LOCAL CARIBBEAN (LOL GLOC@L)
HOME   HERITAGE & TRAVEL   JOURNALISM & COM4DEV   SDG GENDER DEV PLATFORM   CURIOSITY SHOP
EXPLORE! ENTERTAIN! EXCITE! EDUCATE! EMPOWER! ENGAGE! OUR WORLD THROUGH NOVEL LENSES
VIRTUAL TOURS MUSEUM
GALLERIES ARCHIVES
MULTIMEDIA LIFELONG
LEARNING ACADEMY

The ADVENTURES Of
BOOK 3
MUNNIE BUTTERFLY & & DANNY DRAGONFLY
MUNNIE
MultiCultural
Musical
Masquerade
KRIS RAMPERSAD
Subscribe Now www.krisrampersad.com

KnowledgePot
Leaves of Life
LEAVES OF LIFE GLOBAL LOCAL CARIBBEAN (LOL GLOC@L)
HOME   HERITAGE & TRAVEL   JOURNALISM & COM4DEV   SDG GENDER DEV PLATFORM   CURIOSITY SHOP
XPLORE! ENTERTAIN! EXCITE! EDUCATE! EMPOWER! ENGAGE! OUR WORLD THROUGH NOVEL LENSES
VIRTUAL TOURS MUSEUM
GALLERIES ARCHIVES
MULTIMEDIA LIFELONG
LEARNING ACADEMY

BOOK 3 The Adventures of
MUNNIE BUTTERFLY
& DANNY DRAGONFLY

Danny is flittering a mile a minute. "We are going to be dragon food!" he warns.

Munnie does not see the dragon but she sees the colourful band of ferocious cats poised to pounce. "They look hungry" Danny shouts. The little butterfly and dragonfly freeze in mid-air as the monsters make ready for the midday meal…

MUNNIE MultiCultural Musical Masquerade

www.krisrampersad.com
GET THE FULL SERIES in musical audiobook & animated video formats with fun learning tools.